Mr. Kris Kringle
A Christmas Tale

S. Weir Mitchell

Contents

MR. KRIS KRINGLE
A CHRISTMAS TALE

BY

S. Weir Mitchell

MR. KRIS KRINGLE.
A
Christmas Tale.
BY
S. WEIR MITCHELL, M. D., LL. D., HARVARD.

*   *   *   *   *

The following little Christmas story was written, and is   published for the benefit of the Home of the Merciful Saviour   for Crippled Children, Philadelphia.

S. WEIR MITCHELL.

*   *   *   *   *

MR. KRIS KRINGLE.

It was Christmas Eve. The snow had clad the rolling hills in white, as if in preparation for the sacred morrow. The winds, boisterous all day long, at fall of night ceased to roar amidst the naked forest, and now, the silent industry of the falling flakes made of pine and spruce tall white tents. At last, as the darkness grew, a deepening stillness came on hill and valley, and all nature seemed to wait expectant of the coming of the Christmas time.

Above the broad river a long, gray stone house lay quiet; its vine and roof heavy with the softly-falling snow, and showing no sign of light or life except in a feeble, red glow through the Venetian blinds of the many windows of one large room. Within, a huge fire of mighty logs lit up with distinctness only the middle space, and fell with variable illumination on a silent group about the hearth.

On one side a mother sat with her cheek upon her hand, her elbow on the table, gazing steadily into the fire; on the other side were two children, a girl and a boy; he on a cushion, she in a low chair. Some half-felt sadness repressed for these little ones the usual gay Christmas humor of the hopeful hour, commonly so full for them of that anticipative joy to which life brings shadowy sadness as the years run on.

Now and then the boy looked across the room, pleased when the leaping flames sent flaring over floor and wall long shadows from the tall brass andirons or claw-footed chair and table. Sometimes he glanced shyly at the mother, but getting no answering smile kept silence. Once or twice the girl whispered a word to him, as the logs fell and a sheet of flame from the hickory and the quick-burning birch set free the stored-up sunshine of many a summer day. A moment later, the girl caught the boy's arm.

"Oh! hear the ice, Hugh," she cried, for mysterious noises came up from the river and died away.

"Yes, it is the ice, dear," said the mother. "I like to hear it." As she spoke she struck a match and lit two candles which stood on the table beside her.

For a few minutes as she stood her gaze wandered along the walls over the portraits of men and women once famous in Colonial days. The great china bowls, set high for safety on top of the book-cases, tankards, and tall candelabra troubled her with memories of more prosperous times. Whatever emotions these relics of departed pride and joy excited, they left neither on brow nor on cheek the unrelenting signals of life's disasters. A glance distinctly tender and distinctly proud made sweet her face for a moment as she turned to look upon the children.

The little fellow on the cushion at her feet looked up.

"Mamma, we do want to know why Christmas comes only once a year?"

"Hush, dear, I cannot talk to you now; not to-night; not at all, to-night."

"But was not Christ always born?" he persisted.

"Yes, yes," she replied. "But I cannot talk to you now.

Be quiet a little while. I have something to do," and so saying, she drew to her side a basket of old letters.

The children remained silent, or made little signs to one another as they watched the fire. Meanwhile the mother considered the papers, now with a gleam of anger in her eyes, as she read, and now with a momentary blur of tear-dimmed vision. Most of the letters she threw at once on the fire. They writhed a moment like living creatures, and of a sudden blazed out as if tormented into sudden confession of the passions of years gone by; then they fell away to black unmemoried things, curling crumpled in the heat.

The children saw them burn with simple interest in each new conflagration. Something in the mother's ways quieted them, and they became intuitively conscious of sadness in the hour and the task. At last the boy grew uneasy at the long repose of tongue.

"O Alice! see the red sparks going about," he said, looking at the wandering points of light in the blackening scrolls of shrivelled paper.

"Nurse says those are people going to church," said his sister, authoritatively.

Her mother looked up, smiling. "Ah, that is what they used to tell me when I was little."

"They're fire-flies," said the boy, "like in a vewy dark night." Now and then his r's troubled him a little, and conscious of his difficulty, he spoke at times with oddly serious deliberation.

"You really must be quiet," said the mother. "Now, do keep still, or you will have to go to bed," and so saying she turned anew to the basket.

Presently the girl exclaimed, "Why do you burn the letters?" She had some of her mother's persistency, and was not readily controlled. This time the mother made no reply. A sharp spasm of pain went over her features. Looking into the fire, as if altogether unconscious of the quick spies at her side, she said aloud, "Oh! I can no more! Let them wait. What a fool I was. What a fool!" and abruptly pushed the basket aside.

The little fellow leaped up and cast his arms about her while his long, yellow hair fell on her neck and shoulder. "O Mamma!" he cried, "don't read any more. Let me burn them. I hate them to hurt you."

She smiled on him through tears--rare things for

her. "Every one must bear his own troubles, Hugh. You couldn't help me. You couldn't know, dear, what to burn."

"But I know," said the girl, decisively. "I know. I had a letter once; but Hugh never had a letter. I wish Kris Kringle would take them away this very, very night; and lessons, too, I do. What will he bring us for Christmas, mamma? I know what. I want"--

"A Kris Kringle to take away troubles would suit me well, Alice; I could hang up a big stocking."

"And I know what I want," said the boy. "Nurse says Kris has no money this Christmas. I don't care." But the great blue eyes filled as he spoke.

The mother rose. "There will be no presents this year, Hugh. Only--only more love from me, from one another; and you must be brave and help me, because you know this is not the worst of it. We are to go away next week, and must live in the town. You see, dears, it can't be helped."

"Yes," said Hugh, thoughtfully, "it can't be helped, Alice."

"I don't want to go," said the girl.

"Hush," said Hugh.

"And I do want a doll."

"I told you to be quiet, Alice," returned the mother, a rising note of anger in her voice. In fact, she was close upon a burst of tears, but the emotions are all near of kin and linked in mystery of relationship. Pity and love for the moment became unreasoning wrath. "You are disobedient," she continued.

"O mamma! we are vewy sorry," said the lad, who had been the less offending culprit.

"Well, well. No matter. It is bed-time, children. Now to bed, and no more nonsense. I can't have it, I can't bear it."

The children rose submissively, and, kissing her, were just leaving the room, when she said: "Oh! but we must not lose our manners. You forget."

The girl, pausing near the doorway, dropped a courtesy.

"That wasn't very well done, Alice. Ah! that was better."

The little fellow made a bow quite worthy of the days of minuet and hoop, and then, running back, kissed the tall mother with a certain passionate tenderness, saying, softly, "Now, don't you cry when we are gone, dear, dear mamma," and then, in a whisper, "I will pway God not to let you cwy," and so fled away, leaving her still perilously close to tears. Very soon, up-stairs, the old nurse, troubled by the children's disappointment, was assuring them with eager mendacity that Kris would be certain to make his usual visit, while down-stairs the mother walked slowly to and fro. She had that miserable gift, an unfailing memory of anniversaries, and now, despite herself, the long years rolled back upon her, so that under the sad power of their recurrent memories she seemed a helpless prey.

While the children were yet too young to recognize their loss the great calamity of her life had come. Then by degrees the wreck of her fortune had gone to pieces, and now at last the home of her own people, deeply mortgaged, was about to pass from her forever. Much that was humbling had fallen to her in life, but nothing as sore as this final disaster. At length she rose, took a lighted candle from the table, and walked slowly around the great library room. The sombre bindings of the books her childhood knew called back dim recollections. The great china bowls, the tall silver tankards, the shining sconces, and above, all the Stuart portraits or the Copleys of the men who shone in Colonial days and helped to make a more than imperial nation, each and all disturbed her as she gazed. At last, she returned to the fireside, sat down and began anew her unfinished task. With hasty hands she tumbled over the letters, and at length came upon a package tied with a faded ribbon; one of those thin orange-colored silk bands with which cigars are tied in bundles. She threw it aside with a quick movement of disdain, and opened the case of a miniature, slowly, and with deliberate care. A letter fell on to her lap as she bent over the portrait of a young man. The day, the time, the need to dispose of accumulated letters, had brought her to this which she meant to be a final settlement of one of life's grim accounts. For awhile, she steadily regarded the relics of happier hours. Then, throwing herself back in her chair, she cried aloud, "How long I hoped; how hopeless was my hope, and he said, he said, I was cruel and hard. That I loved him no more. Oh! that was a lie! a bitter lie! But a sot, a sot, and my children to grow up and see what I saw, and learn to bear what I have borne. No! no! a thousand times no! I chose between two duties, and I was right. I was the man of the two, and I sent him away--forever. He said,--yes, I was right, but, my God! how cruel is life! I would never have gone, never! never! There!" she exclaimed, and threw back the miniature into the basket, closing it with violence, as she did so, as one may shut an unpleasant book read and done with.

For a moment, and with firmer face, she considered the letter, reading scraps of it aloud, as if testing her resolution to make an end of it all. "Hard, was I? Yes. Would I had been sooner hard. My children would have been better off. 'I went because you bid me.' Yes I did. Will he ever know what that cost me? 'I shall never come again until you bid me come.' Not in this world then?" she cried. "O Hugh! Hugh!" And in a passion of tears that told of a too great trial, still resolute despite her partial defeat, she tore the letter and cast it on the fire. "There!" she cried, "would to God I loved him less." And then, with strange firmness, she took up a book, and sternly set herself to comprehend what she read.

The hours went by and at last she rose wearily, put out one candle, raked ashes over the embers, and taking the other light, went slowly up to bed. She paused a moment at the nursery door where she heard voices. "What! awake still?"

"We was only talking about Khwis," said the small boy. "We won't any more, will we, Alice? She thinks he won't come, but I think he will come because we are both so good all to-day."

"No, no, he will not come this Christmas, my darlings. Go to sleep. Go to sleep," and with too full a heart she turned away.

But the usual tranquil slumber of childhood was not theirs. The immense fact that they were soon to leave their home troubled the imaginative little man. Then, too, a great wind began to sweep over the hills and to shake the snow-laden pines. On its way, it carried anew from the ice of the river wild sounds of disturbance and at last, in the mid hours of night, an avalanche of snow slid from the roof. Hugh sat up; he realized well enough what had happened. But presently the quick ear of childhood was aware of other, and less familiar sounds.

Was it Kris Kringle? Oh! if he could only see him once! He touched the sister asleep in her bed near by, and at last shook her gently.

"What is it, Hugh?" she said.

"I hear Khwis. I know it is Khwis!"

"O Hugh! I hear too, but it might be a robber."

"No, nevah on Chwistmas Eve. It couldn't be a wobber. It is Khwis. I mean to go and see. I hear him outside. You know, Alice, there is nevah, nevah any wickedness on Chwistmas Eve."

"But if it is a robber he might take you away."

"Oh! wobbers steal girls, but they nevah, nevah steal boys, and you needn't go."

"But are you sure? Oh! do listen," she added. Both heard the creaking noise of footsteps in the dry snow.

"I will look--I must look," cried Hugh, slipping from his bed. In a moment he had raised the sash and was looking out into the night. The sounds he had heard ceased. He could see no one. "He has gone, Alice." Then he cried, "Mr. Khwis Kwingle, are you there? or is you a wobber?" As he spoke a cloaked man came from behind a great pine and stood amid the thickly-fallen flakes.

"Why, that is Hugh," he said. "Hugh!"

"He does know my name," whispered the lad to the small counsellor now at his side.

"And, of course, I am Kris Kringle. And I have a bag full of presents. But come softly down and let me in, and don't make a noise or away I go; and bring Alice."

The girl was still in doubt, but her desire for the promised gifts was strong, and in the very blood of the boy was the spirit of daring adventure. There was a moment of whispered indecision, resulting in two bits of conclusive wisdom.

Said Alice, "If we go together, Hugh, and he takes one, the other can squeal. Oh! very loud like a bear- -a big bear."

"And," said Hugh, "I will get my gweat gwandpapa's sword." And with this he got upon a chair and by the failing light of the nursery fire carefully took down from over the chimney the dress rapier which had figured at peaceful levees of other days. "Now," he said, "if you are afwaid I will go all alone myself."

"I am dreadfully afraid," said she, "but I will go, too." So she hastily slipped on a little white wrapper and he his well-worn brown velvet knickerbocker trousers. Neither had ever known a being they had reason to fear, and so, with beating hearts, but brave enough, they stole quietly out in their sweet innocence and hand in hand went down the dark staircase, still hearing faint noises as they felt their way. They crossed the great warm library and entered the hall, where, with much effort, they unlocked the door and lifted the old-fashioned bar which guarded it. The cold air swept in, and before them was a tall man in a cloak half white with snow. He said at once, "Oh! Hugh! Alice! Pleasant Christmas to you. Let us get in out of the cold; but carefully--carefully, no sound!" As he spoke he shut the door behind him. "Come," he said, and seeming to know the way, went before them into the library.

"Oh! I'm so frightened," said Alice to Hugh in a whisper. "I wish I was in bed."

Not so the boy. The man pushed away the ashes from the smouldering logs, and took from the wood basket a quantity of birch bark and great cones of the pine. As he cast them on the quick embers a fierce red blaze went up, and the room was all alight. And now he turned quickly, for Hugh, of a mind to settle the matter, was standing on guard between him and the door to the stairway, which they had left open when they came down. The man smiled as he saw the lad push his sister back and come a step or two forward. He made a pretty picture in his white shirt, brown knee-breeches, and little bare legs, the yellow locks about his shoulders, the rapier in his hand, alert and quite fearless.

"My sister thinks perhaps you are a wobber, sir; but I think you are Mr. Khwis Kwingle."

"Yes, I am Kris Kringle to-night, and you see I know your names--Alice, Hugh." His cloak fell from him, and he stood smiling, a handsome Chris. "Do not be afraid. Be sure I love little children. Come, let us talk a bit."

"It's all wite, Alice," said the boy. "I said he wasn't a wobber."

And they went hand in hand toward the fire, now a brilliant blaze. The man leaned heavily upon a chair back, his lips moving, a great stir of emotion shaking him as he gazed on the little ones. But he said again, quickly:

"Yes, yes, I'm Kris Kringle," and then, with much

amusement, "and what do you mean to do with your sword, my little man?"

"It was to kill the wobber, sir; but you mustn't be afraid, because you're not a wobber."

"And he really won't hurt you," added Alice.

"Good gracious!" exclaimed Kris, smiling, "you're a gallant little gentleman. And you have been--are you always a good boy to--your mother?"

"I has been a vewy good boy." Then his conscience entered a protest, and he added: "for two whole days. I'll go and ask mamma to come and tell you."

"No, no," said Kris. "It is only children can see me. Old folks couldn't see me."

"My mother is vewy young."

"Oh! but not like a child; not like you."

"Please, sir, do let us see the presents," said Alice, much at her ease. For now he pushed a great chair to the fire, and seated them both in it, saying: "Ah! the poor little cold toes." Then he carefully closed the door they had left open, and said, smiling as he sat down opposite them: "I have come far--very far--to see you."

"Has you come far to-night?" said the little host, with

rising courage.

"No, not far to-night." Then he paused. "Is--is your mother--well?"

"Yes," said Hugh, "she is vewy well, and we are much obliged."

"May we soon see the presents?" said Alice. "They did say you would not come to-night because we are poor now."

"And," added Hugh, "my pony is sold to a man, and his tail is vewy long, and he loves sugar--the pony, I mean; and mamma says we must go away and live in the town."

"Yes, yes," said Kris. "I know."

"He knows," said Hugh.

"Oh! they know everything in fairyland," said Alice.

"Was you evah in faywyland, sir?" asked Hugh.

"Yes."

"Where 'bouts is it, sir, and please how is it bounded on the north? And what are the pwincipal wivers? We might look for it on the map."

"It is in the Black Hills."

"Oh! the Black Hills," said Alice. "I know."

"Yes, but you're not sleepy? Not a bit sleepy?"

"No, no."

"Then before the pretty things hop out of my bag let me tell you a story," and he smiled at his desire to lengthen a delicious hour.

"I would like that."

"And I hope it won't be very, very long," said Alice, on more sordid things intent.

"That's the way with girls, Mr. Kwingle; they can't wait."

"Ah, well, well. Once on a time there was a bad boy, and he was very naughty, and no one loved him because he spent love like money till it was all gone. When he found he had no more love given him, he went away, and away, to a far country."

"Like the man in the Bible," said Hugh, promptly. "The--the--what's his name, Alice?"

"The prodigal son," said Kris, "you mean--"

"Yes, sir. The pwodigal son."

"Yes, like the prodigal son."

"Well, at last he came to the Black Hills, and there

he lived with other rough men."

"But you did say he was a boy," said Alice, accurately critical.

"He was gwowed up, Alice. Don't you int--inter--"

"Interrupt, you goosey," said Alice.

"One Christmas Eve these men fell to talking of their homes, and made up their minds to have a good dinner. But Hugh--"

"Oh!" exclaimed the lad, "Hugh!"

Mr. Chris nodded and continued. "But Hugh felt very weak because he was just getting well of a fever, yet they persuaded him to come to table with the rest. One man, a German, stood up and said, 'This is the eve of Christmas. I will say our grace what we say at home.' One man laughed, but the others were still. Then the German said,

'Come, Lord Christ, and be our guest,   Take with us what Thou hast blest.'

When Hugh heard the words the German said he began to think of home and of many Christmas eves, and because he felt a strangeness in his head, he said, 'I'm not well; I will go into the air.' As he moved, he saw before him a man in the doorway. The face of the man was sad, and his garment was white as snow. He said, 'Follow me.' But no others, except Hugh, saw or heard. Now, when Hugh went outside, the man he had seen was gone; but being still confused, Hugh went over the hard snow and among trees, not knowing what he did; and at last after wandering a long time he came to a steep hillside. Here he slipped and rolling down fell over a high place. Down, down, down he fell, and he fell."

"Oh! make him stop," cried little Hugh.

"He fell on to a deep bed of soft snow and was not hurt, but soon got up, and thought he was buried in a white tomb. But soon he understood, and his head grew clearer, and he beat the snow away and got out. Then, first he said a prayer, and that was the only prayer he had said in a long time."

"Oh my!" cried little Hugh. "I did think people could nevah sleep unless they say their prayers. That's what nurse says. Doesn't she, Alice?"

And just here Kris had to wipe his eyes, but he took the little fellow's hand in his and went on.

"Soon he found shelter under a cliff, where no snow was, and with his flint and steel struck a light, and made with sticks and logs a big fire. After this he felt warm and better all over and fell asleep. When he woke up it was early morning, and looking about, he saw in the rock little yellow streaks and small lumps, and then he knew he had found a great mine of gold no man had ever seen before. By and by he got out of the valley and found his companions, and in the spring he went to his mine, which, because he had found it, was all his own, and he got people to work there and dig out the gold. After that he was no longer poor, but very, very rich."

"And was he good then?" said Hugh.

"And did he go home," said Alice, "and buy things?"

"Yes, he went. One day he went home and at night saw his house and little children, and--but he will not stay, because there is no love waiting in his house, and all the money in the world is no good unless there is some love too. You see, dear, a house is just a house of brick and mortar, but when it is full of love, then it is a home."

"I like that man," said Hugh. "Tell me more."

"But first," said Alice, "oh! we do want to see all our presents."

"Ah, well. That is all, I think; and the presents. Now for the presents." Then he opened a bag and took out first a string of great pearls, and said, as he hung them around Alice's neck, "There, these the oysters made for you years ago under the deep blue sea. They are for a wedding gift from Chris. They are too fine for a little maid. No Queen has prettier pearls. But when you are married and some one you love vexes you or is unkind, look at these pearls, and forgive, oh! a hundred times over; twice, thrice, for every pearl, because Kris said it. You won't understand now, but some day you will."

"Yes, sir," said Alice, puzzled, and playing with the pearls.

Said Hugh, "You said, Mr. Khwis, that the oysters make pearls. Why do the oysters make pearls?"

"I will tell you," replied Kris. "If a bit of something rough or sharp gets inside the oyster's house, and it can't be got rid of, the oyster begins to make a pearl of it, and covers it over and over until the rough, rude thing is one of these beautiful pearls."

"I see," said Hugh.

"That is a little fairy tale I made for myself; I often make stories for myself."

"That must be very nice, Mr. Khwis. How nice it must be for your little children every night when you tell them stories."

"Yes--yes"--and here Kris had to wipe his eyes with his handkerchief.

"Isn't that a doll?" said Alice, looking at the bag.

"Yes; a doll from Japan."

"Oh!" exclaimed Alice.

"And boxes of sugar-plums for Christmas," he added. "And, Hugh, here are skates for you and this bundle of books."

"Thank you, sir."

"And these--and these for my--for Alice," and Kris drew forth a half-dozen delicate Eastern scarves and cast them, laughing, around the girl's neck as she stood delighted.

"And now I want to trust you. This is for--for your mother; only an envelope from Kris to her. Inside is a fairy paper, and whenever she pleases it will turn to gold--oh! much gold, and she will be able then to keep her old home and you need never go away, and the pony will stay."

"Oh! that will be nice. We do sank you, sir; don't we, Alice?"

"Yes. But now I must go. Kiss me. You will kiss me?" He seemed to doubt it.

"Oh! yes," they cried, and cast their little arms about him while he held them in a long embrace, loath to let them go.

"O Alice!" said Hugh, "Mr. Khwis is cwying. What's the matter, Mr. Khwis?"

"Nothing," he said. "Once I had two little children, and you see you look like them, and--and I have not seen them this long while."

Alice silently reflected on the amount of presents which Kris's children must have, but Hugh said:

"We are bofe wewy sorry for you, Mr. Khwis."

"Thank you," he returned, "I shall remember that, and now be still a little, I must write to your mother, and you must give her my letter after she has my present."

"Yes," said Alice, "we will."

Then Kris lit a candle and took paper and pen from the table, and as they sat quietly waiting, full of the marvel of this famous adventure, he wrote busily, now and then pausing to smile on them, until he closed and gave the letter to the boy.

"Be careful of these things," he said, "for now I must go."

"And will you nevah, nevah come back?"

"My God!" cried the man. "Never--perhaps never. Don't forget me, Alice, Hugh." And this time he kissed them again and went by and opened the door to the stairway.

"We thank you ever so much," said Hugh, and standing aside he waited for Alice to pass, having in his child-like ways something of the grave courtesy of the ancestors who looked down on him from the walls. Alice courtesied and the small cavalier, still with the old rapier in hand, bowed low. Kris stood at the door and listened to the patter of little feet upon the stair; then he closed it with noiseless care. In a few minutes he had put out the candles, resumed his cloak, and left the house. The snow no longer fell. The waning night was clearer, and to eastward a faint rosy gleam foretold the coming of the sun of Christmas. Kris glanced up at the long-windowed house and turning went slowly down the garden path.

Long before their usual hour of rising, the children burst into the mother's room. "You monkeys," she cried, smiling; "Merry Christmas to you! What is the matter?"

"Oh! he was here! he did come!" cried Alice.

"Khwis was here," said Hugh. "I did hear him in the night, and I told Alice it was Khwis, and she said it was a wobber, and I said it wasn't a wobber. And we went to see, and it was a man. It was Khwis. He did say so."

"What! a man at night in the house! Are you crazy, children?"

"And Hugh took grandpapa's sword, and--"

"Gweat-gwanpapa's," said Hugh, with strict accuracy.

"You brave boy!" cried the woman, proudly. "And he stole nothing, and, oh! what a silly tale."

"But it was Khwis, mamma. He did give us things. I

do tell you it was Khwis Kwingle."

"Oh! he gave us things for you, and for me, and for Hugh, and he gave me this," cried Alice, who had kept her hand behind her, and now threw the royal pearls on the bed amid a glory of Eastern scarves.

"Are we all bewitched?" cried the mother.

"Oh! and skates, and sugar-plums, and books, and a doll, and this for you. Oh! Khwis didn't forget nobody, mamma."

The mother seized and hastily opened the blank envelope which the boy gave her.

"What! what!" she cried, as she stared at the inclosure; "is this a jest?"

UNION TRUST CO., NEW YORK.

MADAME:--We have the honor to hold at your disposal the   following registered United States bonds, in all amounting   to ----.

The sum was a great fortune. The Trust Company was known to her, even its president's signature.

"What's the matter, mamma," cried Alice, amazed at the unusual look the calm mother's face wore as she arose from the bed, while the great pearls tumbled over

and lay on the sunlit floor, and the fairy letter fell un-
heeded. Her thoughts were away in the desert of her
past life.

"And here, I forgot," said Hugh, "Mr. Khwis did write
you a letter."

"Quick," she cried. "Give it to me." She opened it
with fierce eagerness. Then she said, "Go away, leave me
alone. Yes, yes, I will talk to you by and by. Go now."
And she drove the astonished children from the room
and sat down with her letter.

"DEAR ALICE:--Shall I say wife? I promised to
come no more   until you asked me to come. I can
stand it no longer. I came   only meaning to see the
dear home, and to send you and my   dear children a
remembrance, but I--You know the rest. If in   those
dark days the mother care and fear instinctively set
aside what little love was left for me I do not now won-
der.   Was it well, or ill, what you did when you bid
me go? In   God's time I have learned to think it well.
That hour is to   me now like a blurred dream. To-day
I can bless the anger   and the sense of duty to our
children which drove me   forth--too debased a thing

to realize my loss. I have won   again my self-control, thank God! am a man once more. You   have, have always had, my love. You have to-day again a   dozen times the fortune I meanly squandered. I shall never touch it; it is yours and your children's. And now, Alice,   is all love dead for me? And is it Yes or No? And shall I   be always to my little ones Kris, and to-night a mysterious   memory, or shall I be once more

                                        YOUR HUGH?

"A letter to the bank will find me."

As she read, the quick tears came aflood. She turned to her desk and wrote in tremulous haste, "Come, come at once," and ringing for the maid, sent it off to the address he gave. The next morning she dressed with unusual care. At the sound of the whistle of the train she went down to the door. Presently, a strong, erect, eager man came swiftly up the pathway. She was in his arms a minute after, little Hugh exclaiming, "O Alice! Mr. Khwis is kissing mamma!"

                *   *   *   *   *

The Codes Of Hammurabi And Moses
W. W. Davies

QTY

The discovery of the Hammurabi Code is one of the greatest achievements of archaeology, and is of paramount interest, not only to the student of the Bible, but also to all those interested in ancient history...

Religion   **ISBN:** *1-59462-338-4*   **Pages:132**
MSRP $12.95

The Theory of Moral Sentiments
Adam Smith

QTY

This work from 1749. contains original theories of conscience amd moral judgment and it is the foundation for systemof morals.

Philosophy   **ISBN:** *1-59462-777-0*   **Pages:536**
MSRP $19.95

Jessica's First Prayer
Hesba Stretton

QTY

In a screened and secluded corner of one of the many railway-bridges which span the streets of London there could be seen a few years ago, from five o'clock every morning until half past eight, a tidily set-out coffee-stall, consisting of a trestle and board, upon which stood two large tin cans, with a small fire of charcoal burning under each so as to keep the coffee boiling during the early hours of the morning when the work-people were thronging into the city on their way to their daily toil...

Pages:84

Childrens   **ISBN:** *1-59462-373-2*   *MSRP $9.95*

My Life and Work
Henry Ford

QTY

Henry Ford revolutionized the world with his implementation of mass production for the Model T automobile. Gain valuable business insight into his life and work with his own auto-biography... "We have only started on our development of our country we have not as yet, with all our talk of wonderful progress, done more than scratch the surface. The progress has been wonderful enough but..."

Pages:300

Biographies/   **ISBN:** *1-59462-198-5*   *MSRP $21.95*

The Art of Cross-Examination
Francis Wellman

QTY

I presume it is the experience of every author, after his first book is published upon an important subject, to be almost overwhelmed with a wealth of ideas and illustrations which could readily have been included in his book, and which to his own mind, at least, seem to make a second edition inevitable. Such certainly was the case with me; and when the first edition had reached its sixth impression in five months, I rejoiced to learn that it seemed to my publishers that the book had met with a sufficiently favorable reception to justify a second and considerably enlarged edition. ..

Reference   **ISBN: *1-59462-647-2***

Pages:412

MSRP $19.95

On the Duty of Civil Disobedience
Henry David Thoreau

QTY

Thoreau wrote his famous essay, On the Duty of Civil Disobedience, as a protest against an unjust but popular war and the immoral but popular institution of slave-owning. He did more than write—he declined to pay his taxes, and was hauled off to gaol in consequence. Who can say how much this refusal of his hastened the end of the war and of slavery ?

Law   **ISBN: *1-59462-747-9***

Pages:48

MSRP $7.45

Dream Psychology Psychoanalysis for Beginners
Sigmund Freud

QTY

Sigmund Freud, born Sigismund Schlomo Freud (May 6, 1856 - September 23, 1939), was a Jewish-Austrian neurologist and psychiatrist who co-founded the psychoanalytic school of psychology. Freud is best known for his theories of the unconscious mind, especially involving the mechanism of repression; his redefinition of sexual desire as mobile and directed towards a wide variety of objects; and his therapeutic techniques, especially his understanding of transference in the therapeutic relationship and the presumed value of dreams as sources of insight into unconscious desires.

Psychology   **ISBN: *1-59462-905-6***

Pages:196

MSRP $15.45

The Miracle of Right Thought
Orison Swett Marden

QTY

Believe with all of your heart that you will do what you were made to do. When the mind has once formed the habit of holding cheerful, happy, prosperous pictures, it will not be easy to form the opposite habit. It does not matter how improbable or how far away this realization may see, or how dark the prospects may be, if we visualize them as best we can, as vividly as possible, hold tenaciously to them and vigorously struggle to attain them, they will gradually become actualized, realized in the life. But a desire, a longing without endeavor, a yearning abandoned or held indifferently will vanish without realization.

Self Help   **ISBN: *1-59462-644-8***

Pages:360

MSRP $25.45

QTY

The Rosicrucian Cosmo-Conception Mystic Christianity *by Max Heindel*   ISBN: *1-59462-188-8*   **$38.95**
The Rosicrucian Cosmo-conception is not dogmatic, neither does it appeal to any other authority than the reason of the student. It is: not controversial, but is: sent forth in the, hope that it may help to clear...   New Age/Religion Pages 646

Abandonment To Divine Providence *by Jean-Pierre de Caussade*   ISBN: *1-59462-228-0*   **$25.95**
"The Rev. Jean Pierre de Caussade was one of the most remarkable spiritual writers of the Society of Jesus in France in the 18th Century. His death took place at Toulouse in 1751. His works have gone through many editions and have been republished...   Inspirational/Religion Pages 400

Mental Chemistry *by Charles Haanel*   ISBN: *1-59462-192-6*   **$23.95**
Mental Chemistry allows the change of material conditions by combining and appropriately utilizing the power of the mind. Much like applied chemistry creates something new and unique out of careful combinations of chemicals the mastery of mental chemistry...   New Age Pages 354

The Letters of Robert Browning and Elizabeth Barret Barrett 1845-1846 vol II   ISBN: *1-59462-193-4*   **$35.95**
by Robert Browning and Elizabeth Barrett   Biographies Pages 596

Gleanings In Genesis (volume I) *by Arthur W. Pink*   ISBN: *1-59462-130-6*   **$27.45**
Appropriately has Genesis been termed "the seed plot of the Bible" for in it we have, in germ form, almost all of the great doctrines which are afterwards fully developed in the books of Scripture which follow...   Religion/Inspirational Pages 420

The Master Key *by L. W. de Laurence*   ISBN: *1-59462-001-6*   **$30.95**
In no branch of human knowledge has there been a more lively increase of the spirit of research during the past few years than in the study of Psychology, Concentration and Mental Discipline. The requests for authentic lessons in Thought Control, Mental Discipline and...   New Age/Business Pages 422

The Lesser Key Of Solomon Goetia *by L. W. de Laurence*   ISBN: *1-59462-092-X*   **$9.95**
This translation of the first book of the "Lernegton" which is now for the first time made accessible to students of Talismanic Magic was done, after careful collation and edition, from numerous Ancient Manuscripts in Hebrew, Latin, and French...   New Age/Occult Pages 92

Rubaiyat Of Omar Khayyam *by Edward Fitzgerald*   ISBN: *1-59462-332-5*   **$13.95**
Edward Fitzgerald, whom the world has already learned, in spite of his own efforts to remain within the shadow of anonymity, to look upon as one of the rarest poets of the century, was born at Bredfield, in Suffolk, on the 31st of March, 1809. He was the third son of John Purcell...   Music Pages 172

Ancient Law *by Henry Maine*   ISBN: *1-59462-128-4*   **$29.95**
The chief object of the following pages is to indicate some of the earliest ideas of mankind, as they are reflected in Ancient Law, and to point out the relation of those ideas to modern thought.   Religiom/History Pages 452

Far-Away Stories *by William J. Locke*   ISBN: *1-59462-129-2*   **$19.45**
"Good wine needs no bush, but a collection of mixed vintages does. And this book is just such a collection. Some of the stories I do not want to remain buried for ever in the museum files of dead magazine-numbers an author's not unpardonable vanity..."   Fiction Pages 272

Life of David Crockett *by David Crockett*   ISBN: *1-59462-250-7*   **$27.45**
"Colonel David Crockett was one of the most remarkable men of the times in which he lived. Born in humble life, but gifted with a strong will, an indomitable courage, and unremitting perseverance...   Biographies/New Age Pages 424

Lip-Reading *by Edward Nitchie*   ISBN: *1-59462-206-X*   **$25.95**
Edward B. Nitchie, founder of the New York School for the Hard of Hearing, now the Nitchie School of Lip-Reading, Inc, wrote "LIP-READING Principles and Practice". The development and perfecting of this meritorious work on lip-reading was an undertaking...   How-to Pages 400

A Handbook of Suggestive Therapeutics, Applied Hypnotism, Psychic Science   ISBN: *1-59462-214-0*   **$24.95**
by Henry Munro   Health/New Age/Health/Self-help Pages 376

A Doll's House: and Two Other Plays *by Henrik Ibsen*   ISBN: *1-59462-112-8*   **$19.95**
Henrik Ibsen created this classic when in revolutionary 1848 Rome. Introducing some striking concepts in playwriting for the realist genre, this play has been studied the world over.   Fiction/Classics/Plays 308

The Light of Asia *by sir Edwin Arnold*   ISBN: *1-59462-204-3*   **$13.95**
In this poetic masterpiece, Edwin Arnold describes the life and teachings of Buddha. The man who was to become known as Buddha to the world was born as Prince Gautama of India but he rejected the worldly riches and abandoned the reigns of power when...   Religion/History/Biographies Pages 170

The Complete Works of Guy de Maupassant *by Guy de Maupassant*   ISBN: *1-59462-157-8*   **$16.95**
"For days and days, nights and nights, I had dreamed of that first kiss which was to consecrate our engagement, and I knew not on what spot I should put my lips..."   Fiction/Classics Pages 240

The Art of Cross-Examination *by Francis L. Wellman*   ISBN: *1-59462-309-0*   **$26.95**
Written by a renowned trial lawyer, Wellman imparts his experience and uses case studies to explain how to use psychology to extract desired information through questioning.   How-to/Science/Reference Pages 408

Answered or Unanswered? *by Louisa Vaughan*   ISBN: *1-59462-248-5*   **$10.95**
Miracles of Faith in China   Religion Pages 112

The Edinburgh Lectures on Mental Science (1909) *by Thomas*   ISBN: *1-59462-008-3*   **$11.95**
This book contains the substance of a course of lectures recently given by the writer in the Queen Street Hall, Edinburgh. Its purpose is to indicate the Natural Principles governing the relation between Mental Action and Material Conditions...   New Age/Psychology Pages 148

Ayesha *by H. Rider Haggard*   ISBN: *1-59462-301-5*   **$24.95**
Verily and indeed it is the unexpected that happens! Probably if there was one person upon the earth from whom the Editor of this, and of a certain previous history, did not expect to hear again...   Classics Pages 380

Ayala's Angel *by Anthony Trollope*   ISBN: *1-59462-352-X*   **$29.95**
The two girls were both pretty, but Lucy who was twenty-one who supposed to be simple and comparatively unattractive, whereas Ayala was credited, as her Bombwhat romantic name might show, with poetic charm and a taste for romance. Ayala when her father died was nineteen...   Fiction Pages 484

The American Commonwealth *by James Bryce*   ISBN: *1-59462-286-8*   **$34.45**
An interpretation of American democratic political theory. It examines political mechanics and society from the perspective of Scotsman James Bryce   Politics Pages 572

Stories of the Pilgrims *by Margaret P. Pumphrey*   ISBN: *1-59462-116-0*   **$17.95**
This book explores pilgrims religious oppression in England as well as their escape to Holland and eventual crossing to America on the Mayflower, and their early days in New England...   History Pages 268

QTY

The Fasting Cure *by Sinclair Upton*   ISBN: *1-59462-222-1*   **$13.95**
In the Cosmopolitan Magazine for May, 1910, and in the Contemporary Review (London) for April, 1910, I published an article dealing with my experiences in fasting. I have written a great many magazine articles, but never one which attracted so much attention... New Age/Self Help/Health Pages 164

Hebrew Astrology *by Sepharial*   ISBN: *1-59462-308-2*   **$13.45**
In these days of advanced thinking it is a matter of common observation that we have left many of the old landmarks behind and that we are now pressing forward to greater heights and to a wider horizon than that which represented the mind-content of our progenitors... Astrology Pages 144

Thought Vibration or The Law of Attraction in the Thought World   ISBN: *1-59462-127-6*   **$12.95**

by William Walker Atkinson   Psychology/Religion Pages 144

Optimism *by Helen Keller*   ISBN: *1-59462-108-X*   **$15.95**
Helen Keller was blind, deaf, and mute since 19 months old, yet famously learned how to overcome these handicaps, communicate with the world, and spread her lectures promoting optimism. An inspiring read for everyone... Biographies/Inspirational Pages 84

Sara Crewe *by Frances Burnett*   ISBN: *1-59462-360-0*   **$9.45**
In the first place, Miss Minchin lived in London. Her home was a large, dull, tall one, in a large, dull square, where all the houses were alike, and all the sparrows were alike, and where all the door-knockers made the same heavy sound... Childrens/Classic Pages 88

The Autobiography of Benjamin Franklin *by Benjamin Franklin*   ISBN: *1-59462-135-7*   **$24.95**
The Autobiography of Benjamin Franklin has probably been more extensively read than any other American historical work, and no other book of its kind has had such ups and downs of fortune. Franklin lived for many years in England, where he was agent... Biographies/History Pages 332

Name	
Email	
Telephone	
Address	
City, State ZIP	

☐ **Credit Card**   ☐ **Check / Money Order**

Credit Card Number	
Expiration Date	
Signature	

Please Mail to: Book Jungle
PO Box 2226
Champaign, IL 61825
or Fax to: 630-214-0564

ORDERING INFORMATION

web*: www.bookjungle.com*
email*: sales@bookjungle.com*
fax*: 630-214-0564*
mail*: Book Jungle PO Box 2226 Champaign, IL 61825*
or PayPal *to sales@bookjungle.com*

Please contact us for bulk discounts

DIRECT-ORDER TERMS

**20% Discount if You Order
Two or More Books**
Free Domestic Shipping!
Accepted: Master Card, Visa,
Discover, American Express

www.ingramcontent.com/pod-product-compliance
Lightning Source LLC
Chambersburg PA
CBHW081203170626
46813CB00009B/3307